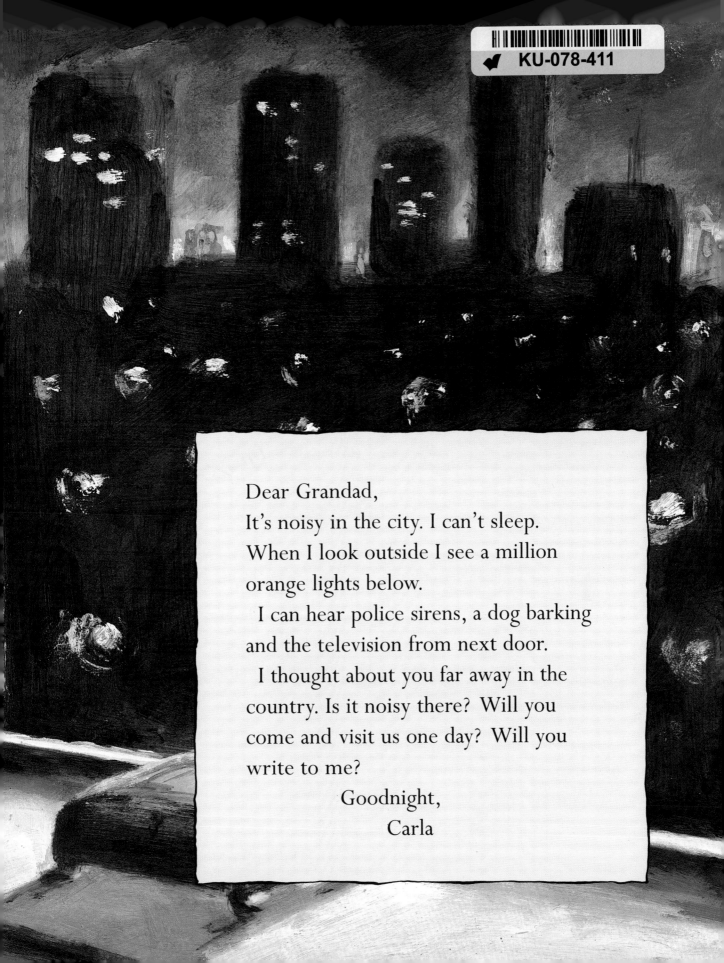

Dear Grandad,
It's noisy in the city. I can't sleep.
When I look outside I see a million
orange lights below.
 I can hear police sirens, a dog barking
and the television from next door.
 I thought about you far away in the
country. Is it noisy there? Will you
come and visit us one day? Will you
write to me?
                    Goodnight,
                    Carla

Dear Carla,
Sometimes I can't sleep either. But it's
the silence that keeps me awake.
    I look out of my window and see the black
shapes of trees, and clouds racing past the moon.
When my eyes become used to the dark, I see
the whole sky is full of stars.
    I think about you too, high up in your flat.
I'd like to visit you one day.
    Send my love to everyone.
                        Grandad

THE MAGPIE SONG

LAURENCE ANHOLT

Illustrated by

DAN WILLIAMS

picture mammoth

Dear Grandad,

I don't like it much at school. I can't do anything right. Today Mum was late to collect me and Mrs Evans was cross.

It was really cold waiting for the bus. It began to snow, but it didn't make the ground all white - just muddy and grey.

At home the lift wasn't working and we had to carry the shopping up all 574 steps to the flat. When we got in, Dad had already gone to work.

Did it snow where you are? Are there any wild animals in the woods?

Love from,

Carla

Dear Carla,

Yes, it did snow here too. I'll tell you about it, but first let's talk about school. If the work you do at school is like the letters you write to me, then you must be clever. Your dad never liked school, but I taught him to carve wood and now he makes some wonderful things. Everyone can do something well. Just remember that.

The woods are like a magic place, as white as the pages of a book. It tells you the whole story of the night before, if you know how to read it. The words are animal footprints. I could see a fox had been hunting and some deer had been in the garden.

There's a family of magpies nesting in a hollow tree by the house. Do you know the song? One for sorrow, two for joy . . . There were three magpies this morning - three for a girl, that's why I thought of you.

Write soon.

Love,

Grandad

Dear Grandad,
There are wild animals in the city too.
Dad told me. He says when you work
nights you see all kinds of things other
people don't. Once he saw rats in the
underground tunnel. Some people sleep
down there too, because they don't have
anywhere to go.

I asked Dad about the Magpie Song,
but he said he didn't remember it. I've
never seen a real magpie.

Dad says he will make me a bird table
for the balcony.

Please come and see me soon.
> Love from,
> Carla

Dear Grandad,
Why haven't you written? It's your
turn to write.
> Carla

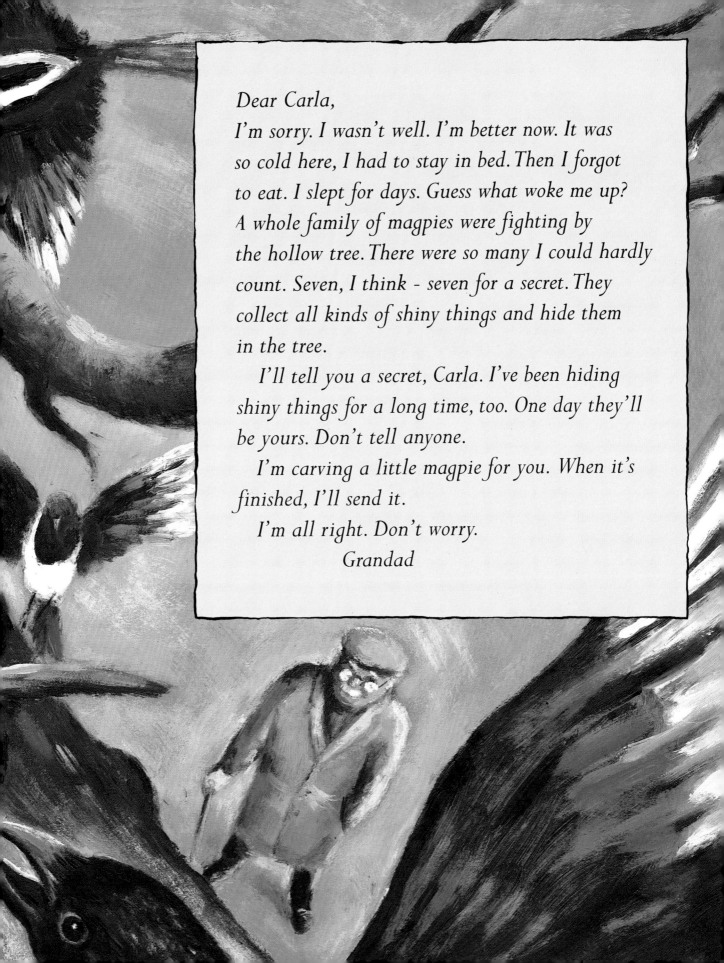

Dear Carla,

I'm sorry. I wasn't well. I'm better now. It was
so cold here, I had to stay in bed. Then I forgot
to eat. I slept for days. Guess what woke me up?
A whole family of magpies were fighting by
the hollow tree. There were so many I could hardly
count. Seven, I think - seven for a secret. They
collect all kinds of shiny things and hide them
in the tree.

I'll tell you a secret, Carla. I've been hiding
shiny things for a long time, too. One day they'll
be yours. Don't tell anyone.

I'm carving a little magpie for you. When it's
finished, I'll send it.

I'm all right. Don't worry.

Grandad

Dear Grandad,
I'm sorry you weren't well. We've got
a secret too! Mum's going to have a baby.
I'm pleased, of course, but it means she
won't be able to work for a long time and
she's worried about the money. Dad
doesn't get much work now either.
    Yesterday Dad took me to see the
lights and look in the shop windows.
They were full of wonderful things.
    Do you think the baby will be a boy?
I don't know where he will sleep.He
will have to share my room.
    I like your secret.
    Please remember to eat.
        Love from,
            Carla

Dear Carla,

Yes! I heard about the baby. I'm so pleased. It will be born in the Autumn. I wish you could all come and live with me. There's plenty of room, but there's no work here for your Dad.

I do want to visit you, Carla, but I'm still not quite fit enough.

I've finished the magpie and now I'll paint it, but not just black and white - magpies have a green and blue sheen when you look at them carefully.

I'll send it soon.

Grandad

Dear Grandad,

Thank you for the magpie. I love it.
I carry it everywhere with me.

Dad has been home all week. He seems
so sad. He says there are too many bills
to pay.

I asked him about when he was a boy
and he showed me a photo. He had long
black hair, didn't he? He said he used to
run through the woods like a wild animal.
Do you remember?

Today he's been making the bird table.
It's just like a miniature house. I can't
remember your house. Will you tell
me about it?

      Love,

        Carla

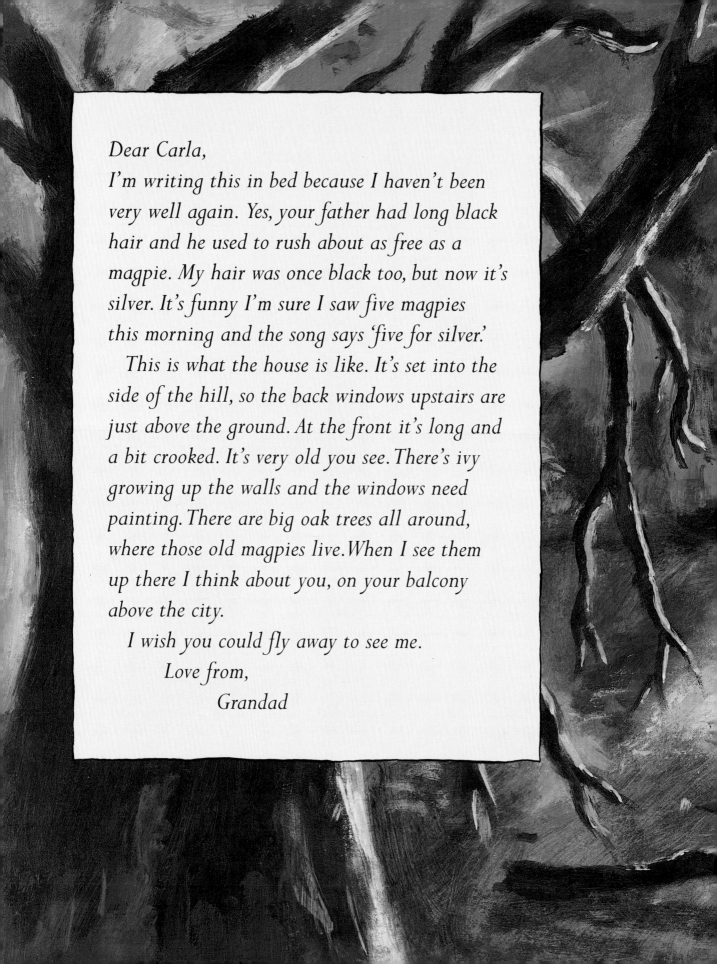

Dear Carla,

I'm writing this in bed because I haven't been very well again. Yes, your father had long black hair and he used to rush about as free as a magpie. My hair was once black too, but now it's silver. It's funny I'm sure I saw five magpies this morning and the song says 'five for silver.'

This is what the house is like. It's set into the side of the hill, so the back windows upstairs are just above the ground. At the front it's long and a bit crooked. It's very old you see. There's ivy growing up the walls and the windows need painting. There are big oak trees all around, where those old magpies live. When I see them up there I think about you, on your balcony above the city.

I wish you could fly away to see me.
Love from,
Grandad

Grandad,

It's summertime now and you still haven't been. I hope you're not ill again? Have you been eating?

Mum and Dad are at home all the time now. Yesterday a letter came. It said they might take the flat away if we don't find some money. I hear Mum and Dad talking about it at night and I get scared for us and the new baby.

The birds have been coming to the table, but there isn't much food for them.

Please write soon.

     Love,

        Carla

Carla,
There were four magpies this morning and
I knew your brother was born.
   The doctor won't let me write any more now.
   Don't forget our secret.
      I love you,
         Grandad

Dear Grandad,
Why don't you write? You promised
to come.
      . . . Carla

Dear Grandad,

Something happened. I woke up early because the baby was crying. I looked out onto the balcony and there was a bird there, a big bird, it looked like a magpie. He looked at me. He seemed hungry. Perhaps he'd flown a long way. Perhaps he'd forgotten to eat.

Then I remembered the magpie song - 'One for sorrow . . .' Grandad I'm sad. You promised to come. Did you send the magpie instead?

Love,

Carla

Dear Grandad,

I don't know why I'm writing. It's just a habit I suppose.

   We love the house. Dad mended the roof and painted the windows. He put the bird table in the garden. He spends a lot of time doing wood carvings now. This morning I heard him singing The Magpie Song.

   I'm older now, but when I run in the woods with my brother I sometimes feel you are here.

   Carla

Dear Carla,

If you're reading this letter, you've found the secret! I knew you would. No one else would look in the magpie tree.

Show the box to your father. I carved six magpies on the lid. You know why.

Be happy,

Grandad

Dear Grandad,

There were two magpies on the bird table.

Thank you,

Carla

For Alison, Nick and Sam – joy for a boy
L.A.

For my wife Jane
D.W.

First published in Great Britain in 1995
by Heinemann Young Books
Published 1997 by Mammoth
an imprint of Egmont Children's Books Limited
239 Kensington High Street, London W8 6SA
10 9 8 7 6 5 4 3
Text copyright © Laurence Anholt 1995
Illustrations copyright © Dan Williams 1995
Laurence Anholt and Dan Williams
have asserted their moral rights

ISBN 0 7497 3027 7

A CIP catalogue record for this title
is available from the British Library

Printed at Oriental Press, Dubai, U.A.E